CHOOSE YOUR OWN ADVENTURE®
titles in Large-Print Editions:

CHOOSE YOUR OWN ADVENTURE® • 117

THE SEARCH FOR ALADDIN'S LAMP

BY JAY LEIBOLD

ILLUSTRATED BY JUDITH MITCHELL

An R.A. Montgomery Book

Gareth Stevens Publishing
MILWAUKEE

For a free color catalog describing Gareth Stevens' list of high-quality books, call 1-800-542-2595 (USA) or 1-800-461-9120 (Canada). Gareth Stevens' Fax: (414) 225-0377.

Library of Congress Cataloging-in-Publication Data available upon request from publisher. Fax: (414) 225-0377 for the attention of the Publishing Records Department.

ISBN 0-8368-1311-1

This edition first published in 1995 by
Gareth Stevens Publishing
1555 North RiverCenter Drive, Suite 201
Milwaukee, Wisconsin 53212 USA

CHOOSE YOUR OWN ADVENTURE® is a trademark of Bantam Doubleday Dell Books for Young Readers, a division of Bantam Doubleday Dell Publishing Group, Inc.

Original conception of Edward Packard.
Interior illustrations by Judith Mitchell. Cover art by James Warhola.

1 2 3 4 5 6 7 8 9 99 98 97 96 95

Printed in the United States of America

THE SEARCH FOR ALADDIN'S LAMP

WARNING!!!

Do not read this book straight through from beginning to end. These pages contain many different adventures that you may have in your search for the legendary Lamp of Aladdin. From time to time as you read along, you will be asked to make a choice. Your choice may lead to success or disaster!

The adventures you have are the results of your choices. You are responsible because you choose! After you make a decision, follow the instructions to find out what happens to you next.

Think carefully before you act. Your vacation in Istanbul, Turkey, can be fun, but it may also be dangerous. Even if you do find Aladdin's Lamp and its magical genie, you may not necessarily be pleased with what you have wished for.

Good luck.

You walk up behind your aunt Millie. She's still studying the same painting that she's been standing in front of for the past half hour now. To you it looks pretty much the same as the hundreds of other paintings your aunt has taken you to see since your arrival in Istanbul a week ago.

The ancient painting shows some men with halos over their heads walking up a mountainside. Their feet, however, don't really seem to be touching the ground—it looks more like they're floating up the mountain, or as if they've been pasted on *top* of the landscape. The colors of the painting are dim, except for the halos, which are a shiny gold leaf. You suppose the artist had to use that to make up for the way the facial features and the bodies of the figures are weirdly elongated and out of proportion.

You start to say something about how it's time to leave, but Millie is in such rapture that you hold your tongue. You shiver in your shirtsleeves. You've looked at all the other paintings in this Byzantine church by now, and you're ready to go. Outside, the temperature must be above ninety. But inside the church, cold drafts creep through the corridors and seep out of the heavy stone walls. It feels as though the musty air hasn't changed for centuries. This was not what you had in mind when you accepted your aunt's invitation to take a trip to Turkey.

"I'm going outside," you finally mumble to your aunt. She nods vaguely in your direction. You wonder whether or not she has even heard you.

Turn to page 2.

2

Wandering down a side aisle, you try to remember how you got to this part of the church. You know you came up at least one flight of stairs, or was it two? Rays of sun come in through stained glass windows, lighting up the dust in the air. One thing you can say for the Byzantines, they sure built enormous churches—huge, silent, and drafty.

Since you've arrived in Istanbul a week ago, you've seen more churches than you care to count. You knew that your aunt Millie was going to write an article about Byzantine painting, but you didn't expect to spend so much time preparing for it, especially after she told you the *real* reason for coming to Turkey—to search for the fabled Lamp of Aladdin.

Millie is your favorite relative. For one thing, she doesn't worry about the nonsense that most grown-ups do, like what other people think of her or whether her shoes match her earrings, things like that. She doesn't wear makeup, and her clothes look as if she's just stepped off a bush plane from Alaska or a barge on the Nile—as if she's just coming back from some adventure.

Which is the other thing you love about Millie— she's a travel writer, and she *is* always just coming back from some kind of adventure. You always make her tell you every detail of her latest trip, especially when she's been to exotic places like Turkey. You've vowed to yourself that when you grow up you're going to be just like her and not like your boring parents.

Go on to the next page.

You remember sitting in your room strumming your guitar one afternoon when Millie called to announce that she'd gotten another assignment. She was going to Istanbul again this summer. Your heart started pumping faster. And when she asked, as you hoped she would, if you wanted to come along, you couldn't get the words out fast enough. "Aunt Millie, I can't wait!"

"Millicent," your mother said sternly on the other line, "I think we'd better discuss this first."

"Mother!" you protested.

"It's one thing for your aunt to go running off to these foreign places," your mother replied, "but I don't want you going and getting blown up by some bomb."

That night Millie came over for dinner and managed to convince your parents that you'd be safe with her. "Turkey is a stable country," she assured your mother. "It's safer in Istanbul than on the streets of most American cities."

But *you* weren't worried about danger. Aunt Millie never lets fear of the unknown stop her, and neither will you. When your parents finally agreed to let you go, you immediately went out and got an after-school job. Millie had a free frequent-flyer airline ticket for you, so all you needed was to earn enough to pay for your expenses while you were in Turkey.

Turn to page 50.

Finally you come to an ancient, thick wooden door with iron braces. The door is open. You start to go through it, but then you halt. The passage beyond is very dim. Hardly anything in front of you is visible, and the air is even colder than before.

You turn to go back up the stairs. "Wait a minute," you say to yourself. "Is this what Millie would do—pass up a chance to explore a secret passage?"

You turn around and venture through the doorway into the dark passage. You have to stoop to get through the low archway. A small, flickering candle set into the wall provides the only light. The candle has burned down to the last quarter inch of its life. You keep going into almost total darkness before you come upon another candle.

Then suddenly you freeze. A noise is coming from behind you. You listen. There it is again—footsteps on the stairs!

Your mind races as you turn back toward the door. Should you let yourself be discovered by whoever is approaching? Or should you close the door and hope that will keep you safe? You listen more closely. The footsteps have a clip-clop cadence, making you wonder if they are human.

If you push the door shut in front of you, turn to page 58.

If you decide to see who is coming down the stairs, turn to page 108.

"For that I am grateful," the queen says. "But how do you propose to free her?"

"I don't know," you say. "Can't we use—what about the lamp?"

"What makes you think we have the lamp?" the queen answers with great reserve. "And even if we did, how would it help us?"

"Well, the genie could get your daughter back," you suggest. "Just rub the lamp, and the genie will come out, or so I've heard."

The queen is silent for a moment. Then she says quietly, "Rub it with what?" If she had eyebrows you're sure they would be arched.

That's something you hadn't thought of. "You begin to see our problem," the queen goes on. "All you humans seem to want the lamp. Indeed, you will go to any lengths to obtain it. But if we were to give it to you, and you were able to summon the genie, you would have complete power over us.

"Our problem is to find a human we can trust," she adds. "How can you prove to us you are worthy of receiving the lamp?"

A lot of answers come to mind, but none of them is good enough. "I cannot," you say honestly.

The queen tilts her head and looks at you. "Now that is an answer I have not heard before." She raises herself to her full height and commands her attendants, "Bring the lamp. We have found a trustworthy human who will help us save the princess."

The lamp is retrieved. It is placed before you, wrapped in silks, on a copper platter.

Turn to page 53.

"Of course I dismissed his offer as a hoax or some sort of trick," Millie added. "But the strange thing is, another man tracked me down at home in the States. He said he represented a group of Sufi mystics, and that if I knew anything about Aladdin's Lamp, he'd like to hear about it."

"What's a Sufi?" you interrupted.

"Sufis are an ancient sect of Muslim mystics. They live mostly in Turkey and Iran. Have you heard of whirling dervishes?"

You nodded, and Millie went on, "Well, they're Sufis. Anyway, that made me think that there might be more to the man's story than I thought."

"Oh, boy!" you exclaimed. "So we're going straight to the Grand Bazaar as soon as we land?"

"No," Millie responded, "we have to be patient. First we'll give whoever is involved in this a chance to come to us. In the meantime, I'll research my article on Byzantine painting. Then, if nothing has happened, we'll go to the bazaar."

That was a week ago. Now, wandering through the dank corridors of the church, you ask yourself when all the adventures are going to begin.

You pass an arched entryway leading to a narrow flight of stone stairs. Thinking they must lead to ground level, you go back and take them downward.

Turn to page 55.

8

To your amazement, the impact never comes. Somehow you have entered your lamp.

You open your eyes again to find yourself floating through a fantastic landscape. You're still falling, but more slowly, as if the air is thicker. Whizzing and floating by you are burning meteors, flaming swords, and sickle moons.

You keep falling in a curious, slow motion. You're able to focus more clearly now on the objects around you. Bouncing and galloping past you are flapping tents, long camel caravans, processions of servants and soldiers, glittering mosques, and every once in a while a plummeting sultan.

Your fall slows down even more as the atmosphere becomes thick, like a heavy liquid. But you don't feel it on your skin. Instead, you now seem to be coming into a more airy realm, where you see soaring eagles with many-colored wings, plumed peacocks, and big piles of clouds that turn into green sapphire mountains and then back again into clouds.

With wide eyes you keep watching as a huge bull with thousands of legs and horns passes by. A gigantic whale breaches and dives, causing everything around you to quake and tremble. Then you see swooping angels, a ruby chair, and finally, a blinding light that causes you to throw your arms up in front of your eyes.

Ever so gently your feet touch ground, and you collapse in a heap.

Turn to page 60.

You keep your head protected, letting the stampede carry you along. Finally the herd veers off, dropping you at the foot of a range of dry, rugged mountains. Following a footpath into the range, you cross pass after snow-covered pass. As you come down a broad river valley, you go by ruined castle battlements built on top of lonely mountain buttes.

You walk along a trickling snowmelt stream that comes down from the mountains. It cuts a canyon out of the plateau around you. You keep following it as it drops deeper and deeper into the canyon cut, so deep that you now see the sun for less than an hour every day. Sentinel spires and rose-colored cliffs tower above you.

One day a rumble comes from the canyon above. Lightning strikes, and it begins to rain.

The rain comes down for three days, soaking you to the bone. You keep walking, but you are overtaken by a deafening roar as a torrential flood sweeps you down the canyon. You struggle to keep your head above the foaming white water, but your strength finally gives out, and you abandon yourself to the deluge.

It takes a while to open your eyelids, which seem glued shut. You find that the flood has deposited you next to a violet pool in a green grotto. A trickling waterfall feeds the pool, which is completely overhung with lavish trees, hedges, and creepers.

Turn to page 59.

10

You allow yourself to wander through the alleys of the bazaar. In one, a row of merchants are purveying fantastical chess sets, pipes, delicately carved boxes, and jewelry. In another you find leather goods of all kinds. A black jacket catches your eye, but when the merchant tells you it's goat leather, you lose interest. You pass other alleys of spices, rugs, scarves, pots and pans, ball bearings—every product imaginable.

As you pass a tiny corner of shops selling papyrus, Millie suddenly cries out, "That's our man!" He sees her at the same moment and puts his finger to his lips, asking her to be discreet.

The merchant greets Millie warmly and takes the two of you into a small back room, plushly appointed with carpets and ottomans. He plies you with thick, sweet coffee laced with cardamom. You talk of this and that, and finally he gets around to asking Millie if she's interested in Aladdin's Lamp.

"I'd like to see it," Millie says demurely.

Turn to page 79.

A tingle of fear and excitement creeps up your spine as you examine the paintings. Your tingle turns to panic, though, when the candles begin to flicker and you realize they, too, are about to go out.

You run out of the chamber, back toward the door, figuring you'd rather deal with some hoofed creature than be trapped here in the dark. You feel your way along the cold stone walls until you arrive at the reassuring solid wood. Something is still pawing at the door. "Let me in," a hoarse voice bleats. You grasp for a handle, but you can find none.

Then you remember the pack of matches Aunt Millie made you include in the travel pouch hanging under your shirt. You fish out the pouch and, with trembling fingers, light one of the matches. You search up and down the door, only to find that it has no handle!

The pawing on the other side has stopped. You drop the match and pound the door with your fists, but it's so heavy it just absorbs the blows.

Dejected, you slump to the floor. Darkness envelops you. You wish your aunt Millie were here with you. Then you remember her spirit of adventure. You get to your feet and, deciding to conserve your matches, feel your way back to the chamber in the dark.

Turn to page 116.

The brown furry creature is the strangest looking genie you've ever seen. You wonder if he really has magical powers. The goat-man seems to believe so. "I have only one wish for you," he says. "I wish to return to my original form."

"You wish to become a goat again?" the *jinn* says.

A look of sadness and longing comes into the goat-man's eyes. "Yes," he says, "I wish to taste the tender grass of Mount Elbistan again."

You can see the goat-man's desire is real, yet you have a hard time understanding it. "You mean you'd rather be a goat than a human?"

The man gives you a long look. "Yes," he says softly. "Life in my human shell has been nothing but suffering."

"No sooner do you wish it than it shall be done," the *jinn* says, and with a flash of smoke both he and the goat-man are gone.

Turn to page 36.

You pick up the zither, which is leaning against the wall. You've never seen anything like it. It's a gorgeous object, inlaid with all kinds of wonderful designs.

You're strangely attracted to it. You can almost hear the strings singing, calling you to sit down and play them.

Or is it just the hissing of the lamp you hear? It's making a noise as if it were giving off steam, although nothing is coming out. You lean closer and realize that the hiss is, in fact, a whispering. Dozens of tiny voices seem to be coming out the spout.

You bolt upright. The whispering is coming not just from the lamp but from the cracks in the stone walls all around you. You start to set the zither aside—but the strings catch your eye again. There's a strange allure about the instrument that makes you want to play it, and yet you're still drawn by the whispering voices of the lamp.

If you start to play the zither, turn to page 62.

If you investigate the whispering voices from the lamp, turn to page 112.

16

You take all of this in quickly, but you still use up half your pack of matches scanning the room. You're going to need a supply of light. You try to think of what you could use for fuel. The perfume wouldn't last very long. Besides, it would be a shame to burn up such fragrant stuff, especially before Aunt Millie has had a chance to try it.

You return to the corner with the musical instruments and strike a match. Something above them catches your eye. Hanging on a hook, almost at ceiling level, is an old copper lamp. Your match goes out. It seems to you, though, that the lamp looks a lot like the one in the painting. You remember with excitement that Aladdin had to climb a ladder to retrieve his lamp from a high wall.

But you have no ladder. How can you reach the lamp?

None of the weapons is long enough. All you can think of is to stack the drums on top of one another and try to climb up them. It seems dangerous, but you don't care. The story of Aladdin and his magic lamp is stuck in your head.

You strike your second-to-last match and move the zither and other musical instruments out of the way so you can get at the drums. It's your lucky day, though—hidden behind the drums is a long pole with a hook on the end.

Turn to page 32.

You mount the staircase as if in a trance. As you expect, there is an opening at the top. But you can't make the last step, which is taller than you are. At that moment a man's turbaned head appears, looking down at you from the opening.

"So there you are!" he exclaims. "What took you so long?" You recognize him as the magician, but he looks different than he did in the chamber. He looks younger.

"Is that the lamp in your hand?" he goes on. "Here, hand it to me. Then I'll help you up the last step."

You lift the lamp up to hand it to him, but as soon as you do, he slaps at it. "What do you take me for, a fool? That's a fake! Where is the real lamp?"

You retreat back down the steps, away from the angry magician. "Come back here, you scoundrel!" he cries. "You think you can steal the lamp and give me a phony one in its place, do you? Well, I'll show you!"

You hear sounds of heavy scraping. A shadow comes over the opening, which is soon blocked off by a stone slab. You're trapped!

But, you remind yourself, there is another lamp in the garden. In the story, Aladdin found his lamp in a recess in the wall at the top of a ladder in the garden.

You go back through the halls of urns and through the garden. The ladder is exactly where it is supposed to be. You set your own lamp down and climb fifty rungs to the top.

Turn to page 33.

You blink once and ask, "Where am I?"

No one answers you at first. Then the magician says, "Why do you pretend not to know? You're here with the rest of the seekers."

"But where is *here*?" you insist.

"What did you seek?" the magician retorts.

"I don't know," you say with a shrug. "The lamp, I guess."

"Well, you've found it," the knight says, gesturing around you, his arms clanking.

"You're inside Aladdin's Lamp," the princess says gently, her voice strangely subdued.

Behind the princess, you notice the Victorian man giving a slight nod at her words. "So some say," the magician remarks.

You sink back on your knees, dumbfounded. "Inside the lamp?! How do I get *out*?" you demand.

The Sufi speaks up in a low, grave voice. "You must dive into your lamp."

You look at him blankly. He points to the walls. You notice that they are curved. The room is oval, and the walls are of smooth, convex metal.

"Climb as far as you can up the wall and dive into your lamp," the Sufi advises.

"That's absurd," you say, looking to the others for support. Their faces tell you little. You wonder what is causing the atmosphere of suspicion and distrust in the room.

Turn to page 113.

20

You set off immediately. Though it seems as if you travel for days, every time you look at Millie in the jewel, she's still searching for you in the church. Only a few minutes seem to have passed for her.

When you grow hungry, you open the pomegranate, take out a seed, and squeeze it. It turns into a feast of cheese, olives, eggs, cucumbers, and tomatoes.

With such good food, you're reluctant to have your journey come to an end. But, with the jewels to guide you, you do finally arrive back in the garden.

You follow the rock passage down toward the underground chamber of the church. You see no sign there of the lamp you and the other seekers were trapped inside. But there is a ladder that rests against the stone wall in front of you.

Your progress up the ladder is slow, as you still have your own lamp in one hand. As you climb its flame seems to grow brighter. At the top of the ladder there is a wooden door. You push it open and find that it leads to a gallery high in the dome of the church.

As you run down a flight of stairs to hunt for your aunt Millie, you wonder how you're going to explain where you've been. You didn't find the Lamp of Aladdin, you reflect, but then again, you did have an adventure. And you still have your own lamp, plus the jewels, which you are sure will come in handy again someday when you really need them—though at the moment you're just not sure when or how.

The End

The queen, a hooded cobra of translucent white crystal, is borne on a silver platter upon the backs of four great pythons. She comes forth to speak to you, her black eyes set off against luminous, quartz-veined skin.

You bow before the queen, then relate your meeting with the brown viper and how you came to be here. She twitches her forked tongue, delicate as a thread, at the mention of her daughter. Her voice is sibilant and musical when she speaks. "My daughter is well, then?"

"Yes, she seemed well," you answer. "Er, except she's still in human form. But that's why I'm here. I wish to help rescue your daughter."

Turn to page 6.

22

You return to the garden. Before anything worse happens, you decide just to get yourself to safety. "I want to go back to Istanbul," you say to the genie with resignation.

He bows. In a flash you are out in the bright sunshine. Just then, enormous black things crash down all around you, nearly crushing you. Quickly you realize the black things are shoe soles, and you are the size of an ant. "Get me out of here!" you yell.

Back in the garden, gasping for breath, you order, "Put me back in Istanbul, regular size."

A second later you're standing on a crowded city sidewalk. People look at you strangely. You look down at yourself, realizing that you are now a goat. "No! Not like this!" you baa.

Once again you are back before the genie, whose lips show the trace of a smirk. Your words come out one at a time, slowly and tersely. "Return me to Istanbul, in my proper size, in my human form, in my present time, AT ONCE!"

The genie rolls his eyes and says, "I wish you'd make up your mind."

Suddenly you are in Istanbul—with a gorgeous view of the city—clinging to the top of a minaret!

You close your eyes, utter a word you're glad no one else can hear, and try to think clearly. It's plain that you're going to have to go to greater lengths to get the genie to do what you want.

"Bring me back!" you cry to the genie. "I promise I'll do anything you want!"

You close your eyes, and a moment later you're clinging to a tree instead of the minaret.

Turn to page 119.

24

You contemplate the various bits of advice you've received. The Sufi's suggestion to dive into your lamp sounds crazy, not to mention foolhardy. Then again, if you really *are* trapped inside Aladdin's Lamp, your situation is already pretty crazy.

The strange thing is, you can't tell what any of their motives are. Why is everyone so secretive and unhelpful? You would think they'd try to work together to free themselves from the lamp. But maybe that's the problem—they're afraid that if they help one another, someone *else* will get the magic Lamp of Aladdin.

In any case, you must decide what to do. You're not sure who to trust, but one thing you know is that if your lamp did have a genie inside, it would solve everyone's problems. Maybe you should try rubbing your lamp again—maybe it *will* work this time.

You wet your fingers and prepare to put out the flame of your lamp. "No!" the Sufi cries out. "Never extinguish your light. That was our mistake!"

Go on to the next page.

You look from the princess to the magician to the knight for guidance. Their faces look expectant, but it's hard to read them clearly. You think they want you to go ahead with your plan, but you can't tell whether it's for your good or for theirs. The Sufi just shakes his head sadly.

You wet your fingers again and hold them poised over the flame as you try to decide what to do.

If you go ahead and extinguish the flame,
turn to page 64.

If you decide not to put it out, turn to page 30.

If you decide to dive into your lamp instead,
turn to page 56.

26

A dark-eyed woman sitting near you, adorned in silks, jewelry, and perfume, lowers her veil and looks at you curiously. She chuckles in a smooth, low voice. "*You* tell *us* what we're doing here. You brought us here," she says, gesturing at the zither.

You look down at the zither, perplexed. Glancing up, you realize that you're no longer in the stone chamber, you're now in a tent. It did seem that you were vocalizing, although what you sang exactly you can't recall.

"You must have had a purpose for summoning us," the woman goes on. "But we can't read your mind. What is it you are looking for?"

"The lamp," you blurt. Everyone waits expectantly, and you go on, "Er, I had this lamp, I mean, I was looking for, well, you know, the Lamp of . . . Aladdin."

Turn to page 37.

You take the pomegranate out of your pocket and threaten the crusader. "Hand over my lamp this instant!"

He lets out a hearty laugh and says, "Sorry, the lamp is mine now!"

You fling the fruit at the knight, but he ducks. It plops harmlessly into the water. He takes two long steps and thrusts a mailed fist into your chest, sending you sprawling onto the bank. Then he jumps into the canoe and pushes off, chortling with glee.

By the time you get to your feet and brush yourself off, the crusader is long gone. You scan the landscape in all four directions, but there is nothing, only the empty, silent horizon.

You have no idea where you are. But you do know it's a long journey back to anyplace familiar—farther than you are ever likely to get.

The End

"Good-bye," you say as you duck low beneath the doorframe. The door makes a ringing sound as it slams shut behind you.

Your lamp lights a dark, upward-sloping, rocky passage. You follow the passage a little way before you see something sparkling up ahead.

You come through an opening, and suddenly you're in a cavernous orchard. The fruit on the trees is all glittering crystals and gems, rubies, sapphires, and jade. A warm, shimmering light suffuses the cavern, dancing in prismatic patterns. At first you can't figure out where the light is coming from; then you realize the source is your lamp, whose flame is being refracted through the thousands of crystal jewels. You have no idea where you are or how these precious stones can grow on trees, but you can't help picking a few and dropping them into your pocket.

At the end of the garden you find a hall where several neatly placed urns sit. You open the lid of one of the urns. At first you think it's empty, but a hissing sound comes from inside. You look closer, only to find it's filled with hundreds of brown vipers, and they're wriggling toward the opening! Quickly you clamp the lid back on.

Moving on through another hall of urns, careful not to knock any over, you arrive at a stone staircase. You have a feeling of déjà vu. This place is exactly like the storybook underground cavern where Aladdin found the lamp!

Turn to page 17.

You pull your hand back from the flame. The diving idea is too absurd for you; and something tells you that it's important to keep your lamp lit. "So you're not going to give it a try?" the magician asks with a hint of disgust.

"Not now," you say quietly.

The people in the room seem to lose interest in you after that. They mill around aimlessly, looking up and down the smooth copper walls of the chamber. You say nothing, warming your hands over the flame of your lamp.

Presently the Victorian adventurer approaches you. "Do you know who I am?" he asks.

Somehow you do. "You're Sir Richard Francis Burton, translator of the *Arabian Nights*," you answer, surprised by your knowledge.

"Do you know why we're all here?" he prompts.

"I can't say as I do," you reply.

"We're here because we would do anything— *anything*—to get our hands on the Lamp of Aladdin. We are prisoners of our own desire." He pauses to let his words sink in. "But you—there's something different about you."

Burton lowers his voice and goes on, "You don't seem to have the same desperate desire to own the lamp. That means there may be a way out for you. It is written that there is a door inside this chamber. We have been unable to find it. But you might, if your motives are pure enough—if you are not consumed by greed for the lamp."

Turn to page 63.

"Well, then, what do you want to do?" Razad demands. "Are you going to go in search of the Lamp of Aladdin, or aren't you?"

"Why do I have to go in search of anything?" you ask. "I don't want to get thrown off the cliff of some castle."

"I don't blame you," the old man says sagely. "The Assassins are strong in their faith. They will die for it."

"What is your purpose, then?" Razad asks you. "If you have no quest to undertake, no mystery to solve, what are we to do?"

"What do you suggest?" you shoot back.

"How can I suggest anything?" she says with an exasperated sigh. "You brought us here. It is you who must tell us what to do."

Turn to page 42.

Lighting your last match, you reach up with the pole and unhook the lamp. You bring it down, and as the match flame starts to burn your fingers, you touch it to the wick of the lamp.

The wick flickers and finally catches. You sigh a deep breath of relief. The fumes from the lamp oil are sweet. You take another whiff and notice they're also a little bit acrid.

You sit down and put your hands around the lamp, feeling the copper begin to warm. You start to rub your hands back and forth, slowly at first, then more briskly. To your disappointment, nothing happens.

You try to be philosophical and tell yourself you didn't really expect anything to happen anyway. Besides, at least now you have some light.

Turn to page 15.

There you find the lamp, hanging on a hook in a recess in the wall. Its flame is still burning, only now it is faint.

As you start to take the lamp off the hook, you feel the ladder move. Then you notice that the hook is attached to a spring, which in turn is attached to the ladder. If you remove the lamp, the spring will release and send you and the ladder plummeting to the ground.

You have an idea. You go back down the ladder and pick up your own lamp. You figure that if you are very careful, you can place yours on the hook at the same moment you remove the Lamp of Aladdin.

You feel a tremor of excitement. The fabled Lamp of Aladdin seems to be within your reach. All you need to do is put out the flame and rub the lamp. If all goes according to legend, a genie who can fulfill your every wish will then appear.

But then you remember Burton's words of caution. Maybe you should not be so eager for Aladdin's Lamp—assuming this is even it.

You sit down to think. It all seems to fit. This *must* be the lamp. Besides, the idea of having a genie to do your bidding is hard to resist. If you don't go for it, you may spend the rest of your life wondering if you missed your big chance.

If you go after the Lamp of Aladdin, turn to page 114.

If you decide to keep your own lamp, turn to page 85.

You can't imagine why the woman in the tree would rather be a cucumber than an eagle—maybe it's just that everyone is most comfortable with what's familiar. "How did you get into this predicament?" you ask.

"I was kidnapped by an evil *jinn*, or genie, as you call it, who wanted me to bear his children. I wouldn't do it, so he turned me into an eagle. Now even my own children do not recognize me," she says sadly. "But if you give me the magic veil, they will see me for who I am and find a way to return me to myself."

You agree to the eagle-cucumber woman's conditions. She says you must also bring provisions of meat and water for her on the long flight, which will take several days. Kogilu goes to fetch them, and soon you are loading your things onto her back. But when Kogilu leads Kyrit toward her, she lets out a shriek. "Surely you're joking! I can't carry all three of you. The horse must stay."

Kogilu stops and folds his arms. "Then I stay, too."

"Kogilu," you say gently, "don't forget you made a promise to undertake this quest with me."

Honor forces Kogilu to relent. He is sullen as he tethers Kyrit to the poplar tree and climbs onto the back of the eagle.

"Don't worry," she says, "when I return I will look after your horse."

Turn to page 74.

The viper's words come back to you: *"The camel will take you there."* The last camel in the caravan is going by; you don't have time to tie your lamp on to its packsaddle. In order to follow the snake's instructions, you will have to leave your lamp behind. Telling yourself the time has come, you reluctantly set it down on the beach.

You fall in alongside the camel, wondering how to mount it. The beast just keeps moving on its path steadfastly, oblivious to you. You grab its packsaddle and try to pull yourself up, only to find yourself on the ground. Finally, as the camel begins to splash into the surf, you grab hold of its tail, and in that way you're able to hitch on to the procession.

Turn to page 48.

Suddenly you're alone. You pick up one of the candles the goat-man has left behind and begin to put the musical instruments back in order.

But you can't help glancing back at the lamp. Setting the candle down, you go and rub the lamp yourself. Once again the mist pours from the spout and the furry *jinn* appears.

"Can I make a wish?" you ask.

"I am only the *jinn* of return," he replies. "I can put you back into any previous form you like. Is there something you would rather be?"

You think for a moment and say, "I guess I'd most like to be like my aunt Millie—except for the writing about paintings and all that."

The *jinn* tilts his head. "But you already are. Otherwise, how would you have gotten here?"

With that, the *jinn* vanishes, and you're left alone with your thoughts once again. Come to think of it, maybe you do have reason to be happy as you are.

The End

You're embarrassed to have said it, so you go on the attack. "What do you mean, I summoned you? I've never met you before in my life—who are you, anyway?"

"I am Razad," the woman answers proudly. "You may not have wished for us, but your song brought us here. You can make us go away, if you like."

A man with deep-set, sun-wizened eyes strokes his thick beard and says, "The Lamp of Aladdin, eh? I always wondered if the stories about that were true. They say there was a king named Aladdin who lived in a castle in a faraway land. The castle sits on top of a mountain, with sheer cliffs on all sides. The king's men were fierce fighters, and loyal like none other. They tell a story of how the king, to impress a visitor, bade two of his men fling themselves off the battlement of the castle. The men jumped, without a moment's hesitation, to their deaths below. They're called Assassins."

Turn to page 67.

"I'm just going to chat with him," you tell the serpent, heading for the bank. "I don't see what harm it can do."

The crusader hails you heartily. "Am I glad to see you! I've been lost for weeks and have not seen another soul for days!"

"I was hoping you could tell me where we are," you say, starting to hand him the paddle.

"Please," the snake hisses vehemently, "take us away from here!"

"What's that?" the crusader cries. "A viper! Kill it!" He draws his sword and slashes into the prow, cutting the snake in two. You try to fend off his next strike with your paddle, but his sword knocks it from your hands. The force of his blow sends the canoe back into the middle of the river, drifting downstream.

The head of the snake, still twitching, speaks to you. You lean forward to hear what he says.

"Take the other piece of my body with you," he whispers. "It will help you breathe when the time comes." After a moment, he adds, "If you are in need of help, open the pomegranate." Another moment passes, and he gasps, "The camel will take you there."

"I'm sorry—" you start to say.

"Do not be sorry," he manages to say. "This is how it is supposed to be. It was written that I would sacrifice my life for the princess. Now it is up to you."

Turn to page 100.

40

You tense for a barbaric attack from the Mongols, but they simply look at you curiously and go on with their business. It appears a raiding party has just brought back a new supply of plunder, and they're too busy enjoying it to worry about a couple of strangers in camp.

Kogilu makes inquiries, and eventually you wend your way to the tent of the great general Balulam. Though occupied with mapping out his next swath of devastation, he is not too busy to receive a pair of strange-looking foreigners.

A jovial, portly fellow, Balulam brings you to his inner tent and invites you to feast on fresh food the likes of which you haven't seen in weeks. His manner is surprisingly poised and gentle, and you wonder if he's really as bad as his reputation.

Once you and Kogilu have stuffed yourselves, you get to the matter at hand. "Do you have the Lamp of Ala al-Din?" you ask him point-blank.

"Why yes, I do," he says. "Let me think . . . Yes, Ala al-Din was the king in the high castle. Poor fellow."

Rather than asking indiscreetly about the previous owner's fate, you go on. "Might it be possible for us to glimpse the lamp—and its powers?"

"Certainly," Balulam replies. Then he pauses and adds, "On one condition. My horse, of whom I am very fond, has taken ill. If you can cure her, I will show you the lamp."

"You must be heartbroken," Kogilu says sympathetically. "We'll do whatever we can."

Turn to page 89.

You follow the viper to a small crevice in the stone walls of the cavern. He slithers right through it. When you wedge yourself into the crevice, it seems to widen to accommodate you. Sliding sideways through the narrow passage, you find it leads out into an underground stream. A canoe sits on the bank of the stream, and the snake slides up to it.

"Here you must pick me up and put me into the boat," he says.

You recoil, but the pitiful look in the snake's beady eyes convinces you to try it. Tentatively you reach out, pick the snake up between two fingers, and keeping him as far away from your body as you can, drop him into the canoe.

"Was that so bad?" he asks in a hurt voice.

You push the canoe into the water and hop in. A paddle is stowed under the seat. The stream goes through a series of phosphorescent caverns, then suddenly breaks out into broad daylight. After a series of small rapids, the stream becomes a slow, serpentine river twisting through a grassy plain.

"Now," the snake says, coiling up in the prow of the canoe, "we can get comfortable and talk."

You take up the paddle and lay it across the gunwale, letting the boat meander along the banks of the sinuous river.

"Let's get right to the point," the viper says. "You tell me what you're after, and I'll tell you what I'm after. I have a feeling we can help each other."

Turn to page 76.

42

A man dressed in skins and leather pushes his way to the front. He has intense black eyes, a thick mustache, and an air of invincibility. Tossing his head back and placing his hand on the hilt of his sword, he proclaims, "I am Kogilu. I will look for the lamp with you. I fear no one."

Some of the people in back cheer this pronouncement. You're sure the Kogilu can live up to his word. Still, you know little about him, and you're not sure you want to take on the long journey and potential danger of searching out Aladdin's Lamp.

On the other hand, you think, it may be the only way to keep peace in the tent. Besides, if the zither really did give you the power to summon this scene, you should be able to change it back when you want to as well.

"Well, why not?" you say, trying to keep things light. "I can always sing my way out of trouble with the zither."

Turn to page 70.

The crusader may be human, but his violence against the snake was needless. You decide to leave him behind. You push off from the bank and try to float away from the knight, but without the paddle you have a hard time controlling the canoe. As the river takes you around a big loop, he runs the short way to cut you off.

"Where are you going?" the crusader yells. "I just saved your life!"

"You didn't save anything, you murderer!" you scream back at him, venting your anger. "I want nothing to do with you."

"Are you insane?" he yells back. "That thing was a viper—a servant of the devil."

"That *thing* was my friend!" you cry. Angrily you try to hand-paddle away from the knight, but the current is strong. As you come around the bend, it takes you right to where he is standing. He jumps down, grabs the prow of the canoe, and drags it ashore.

"Your friend, eh?" he taunts. "I guess you've joined the other side."

Go on to the next page.

"So you *are* another one of the demons that has been vexing me!" he bursts out, drawing his sword. "Infidel!"

You step back, fearing for your life. His zeal seems ridiculous, but it's very real. He charges at you, his sword raised.

Desperately you search for a defense. Your hand finds a lump in your pocket—the pomegranate!

You fling it at the crusader. His sword slices it in

midair, clean in half. Thousands of brown vipers then spring from the seeds inside and chase him, screaming, across the plain.

Turn to page 83.

46

"Thanks anyway," you say to the man, "but I've got to go."

He grabs your arm and fixes you with a fierce look. "Do you mean to tell me you'd pass up a chance at Aladdin's Lamp?"

"Not exactly," you say, squirming. "Just let me go find my aunt Millie. She's really good at these things."

"No!" he bellows. "That would ruin it! You must help me—"

You break his grip and dash out of the chamber, bouncing off the walls of the passage, through the door, and back to the staircase. You hear his clip-clop coming after you from down the corridor, and you run up the stairs two at a time. You check behind you, but the goat-man is no match for your speed.

Turn to page 54.

In the morning you keep your part of the bargain by handing the dagger over to Rukn. He loads you up with provisions and draws you a map showing the plain where Balulam and the Mongols were last seen. You bid him farewell, then set off on the tiny trail down the mountain.

When you get to the bottom, you and Kogilu pore over the map. To your dismay, you see that the scale is very large, and the plain is far away. "If only I had Kyrit," Kogilu says wistfully.

Thinking this may be where your bridle comes in handy, you take it out of your pack. Nothing happens. You throw it to the ground, but still there is nothing. Looking at Kogilu, you shrug, pack the bridle away, and set off on foot.

You travel a long way. It is hot, and though you're glad to have provisions, they also weigh you down. By the time you come to a ridge overlooking the plain, your are about done for.

However, the scene below revives you. Stretching over the plain, as far as your eye can see, is the encampment of Balulam. The plain glistens with sparking gold shields, swords, spears, and saddles. Thousands of men, women, and horses mill about in constant motion. Smoke from their cooking fires drifts lazily into the air. It is at once an awesome, terrifying, and pastoral sight.

Speechless, you and Kogilu can do nothing but walk slowly down into the mass and hope for the best. It occurs to you that your dagger would have done you no good here at all.

Turn to page 40.

The camel caravan walks down into the water and along the bottom of the sea. Pulling the piece of the snake's body from your pocket, you find that by putting it to your mouth, you are provided with oxygen.

You pass through a gate studded with crusty underwater gems. A pair of low iron doors opens into a palace. Still clinging to the camel's tail, you gain entrance with the caravan.

Once inside and out of the water, you let go of the camel and sit up to shake off the seaweed and barnacles attached to your clothes. You can now breathe freely, so you place the piece of the snake back in your pocket. A curious crowd of snakes, large and small, red, brown, and green, has gathered around you. "I am here to see your queen," you announce.

You are taken through the halls of the palace by the assembly of snakes, who make an extraordinary swishing and slithering noise on the marble floors. You pass through a series of jeweled doors, until finally you arrive at the throne of the Serpent Queen.

Turn to page 21.

50

It was during the flight to Istanbul that Millie confided to you that doing an article on Byzantine painting wasn't the only purpose of the trip. "In fact," she said, "it's not even the main purpose." Seeing your eyes light up, she went on, "Do you remember the story of Aladdin's Lamp?"

"Sure," you replied. "Aladdin found a magic lamp, and when he rubbed it, a genie came out. The genie granted Aladdin three wishes."

Millie smiled. "Close enough. I'll tell you the whole story later. Anyway," she said, lowering her voice, "when I was in Istanbul last year, I met a merchant in the Grand Bazaar. He asked me if I was interested in Aladdin's Lamp. I asked him what he meant. He said he could obtain the original Lamp of Aladdin for me."

You raised your eyebrows. Was it possible that the fabled lamp was real? Imagine a genie who could make every wish come true!

Turn to page 7.

He looks sheepish as he answers, "In truth, yes, that is the object I seek. And what a wonderful object it is! More wonderful than the Grail, forsooth. Yet I fear I have become obsessed with its discovery. I have lost my companions, and I have lost my way; indeed, I have sold out everything to find the lamp. Now it is my only hope."

"Why can't you retrace your steps, find your way back, and make a new start?"

"We must find the Lamp of Aladdin," he says with vehemence. "It will solve all of our problems. One cannot just abandon such a quest."

"Right now I'd be satisfied just to get home safely," you say.

"We've got to keep looking!" he insists, clenching a mailed fist. Eyeing your canoe, he says, "Is this craft still seaworthy?"

"As much as it ever was, I suppose."

As you start to climb back into the canoe with him, he notices your lamp, still sitting on the floor of the canoe.

"Why, what's this?" he cries, picking up the lamp. "We are saved!"

Turn to page 118.

The queen fixes you with her beady eyes and says gravely, "The lamp is now in your hands. It is up to you to justify the risk we have taken."

You unwrap the lamp with great care. It has already been emptied of oil. Closing your eyes, you rub it fervently between your hands. A wonderful mist pours from the spout. From out of the mist appears a handsome genie. "You have summoned me, O master," he booms in a sonorous baritone. "Whatsoever you wish, it is my command."

"Go to the chamber in which the daughter of the Serpent Queen is held captive and bring her here to us," you order.

In as much time as it takes to blink, the genie leaves and returns with the princess of the serpents. Back in her snakely form, the princess enjoys a tearful reunion with her mother and all the court.

"You are free to go," the queen says, turning to you. "The lamp is yours."

You thank the queen and wish her and her attendants well. You think for a moment of returning to the copper chamber to show off your find to the captors of the princess. But it is enough to imagine their surprise when she was taken away.

You also consider for a moment leaving the lamp with the Serpent Queen, but you want to see your aunt Millie's face when you show it to her. You're confident you will not abuse it, nor will Millie. It'll be your secret. It will change your lives, but no more than necessary—or so you hope.

The End

Once you make it to the top, you go racing through the church, calling for your aunt. To your dismay, she's still musing over the same painting. You drag her to a quiet alcove and breathlessly relate everything that has just happened. She looks a bit skeptical but allows herself to be led back to the archway that opened onto the staircase.

However, when you get there, the entrance is blocked by a wooden door. "I don't remember seeing this before," you say to Millie. You grab the handle and shake the door. It's locked.

Just then a security guard comes running down the aisle shouting, "Leave that door alone! Visitors are not permitted!"

"Oh well, too bad," Millie says, moving away. "Don't worry, though, we still have our other lead. We'll go to the bazaar first thing tomorrow morning."

You nod, but you can't get the image of what you saw in the chamber out of your mind. Should you accept that you blew your only chance and count on Millie's promise to go to the bazaar tomorrow? Or do you want to insist on trying the door again later?

*If you insist on trying the door again,
turn to page 106.*

If you decide to let it go, turn to page 110.

Maybe Millie's life isn't as exciting as she makes it sound, you think as you descend the stairs. Still, there is the prospect of finding the Lamp of Aladdin. Already you've wasted the first week of your trip looking at paintings. Only three weeks are left.

Over the past few days, Millie has been filling you in on the story of the lamp. First you read the complete tale of Aladdin translated from the original Arabian version of *A Thousand and One Nights*. It was longer and more interesting than you expected. Millie described the long history of storytelling in the Middle East, including Arabic poetry, Turkish epic songs, and the mystical writings of Persia, the old name for Iran.

Millie explained that there have been rumors about the existence of an actual lamp for centuries. "It may not contain a genie like the one in the story. Still, there must be something very special about the lamp," she said. "Otherwise, the Sufis wouldn't be so interested in it."

The lamp has fired your imagination. You can't help but fantasize about finding it for yourself. You're not sure what you'd do with it, but summoning the magical genie would be at the top of the list.

The stairs just seem to keep going down. There haven't been any landings, just the gray stone walls of the spiraling staircase, lit by an occasional dust-covered bulb. It occurs to you that you must have passed ground level a long time ago.

Turn to page 5.

56

Your companions clear a space for you to set your lamp down. As you begin to climb the curved copper wall of the chamber, you feel a little foolish. But now that you've started, you don't want to turn back.

Even though the walls are convex, you're somehow able to get almost halfway to the top, as if you were a fly walking on the ceiling. Crouching on your haunches, you turn around and prepare to dive. But when you look down, you nearly die of fright—suddenly you're thirty feet above the floor. Your lamp is a tiny vessel, with what looks like a furnace burning inside it. The flame-lit faces of your companions looking up at you resemble tiny coins. Only the friction of your soles keeps you from an involuntary plunge.

You can't see any other way down, though, so you stretch your arms in front of you in a diving position, take a deep breath, and jump. A short scream escapes your lips. The faces of the onlookers rush to meet you incredibly fast. You close your eyes and wait for the impact.

Turn to page 8.

58

It takes all your strength to close the heavy wooden door on its hinges. It shuts with a resounding crash. Then you hurry down the passageway. The candles in the wall flicker wildly. Each one is burning the last of its wax as you pass, plunging the corridor behind you into darkness.

You pause to catch your breath. A scratching sound comes from the end of the hall, as if a hoof is pawing at the other side of the door.

The passage bends, and suddenly you find yourself in a small chamber. Set into each wall is a candle. An unusual aromatic scent wafts through the air—a hint of cinnamon, cardamom, and cloves.

Once your eyes adjust to the light, you see that all kinds of curious objects are piled in the corners of the chamber. You also notice that above each candle is a painting. The paintings are unlike any you've seen so far in Istanbul.

The first painting shows an ethereal white horse emerging from a lake. A boy on the bank holds a bridle for the horse. The second painting shows winged serpents, wolves dripping blood from their fangs, cats with elephant trunks, and all kinds of hideous demons tearing the same boy to pieces. The third shows him bent down with his head on a wooden block, an executioner about to bring his sword down.

Turn to page 12.

Above you, on a promontory near the waterfall, is a small stone temple overgrown with vines and moss. You find some steps, half-covered by leaves and dirt, leading up to the top.

As you climb, you see that the landscape around the grotto is far from calm. The sky is tinged orange with flames. A roar like a huge burning furnace reaches your ears, yet you feel no heat.

As a matter of fact, it occurs to you that the temperature of the air is perfect, matched exactly to your body. You feel it with your skin, marveling at how much pleasure you can get from a simple thing like the relative warmth of the air. It's more than just air, though, you realize; it's a sweet, honey-scented medium that you are able to move through with ease. Taking a deep breath, you find that it smells delicious, the most delicate fragrance you can imagine. You taste it, feeling it not only in your lungs, but in every cell in your body.

Turn to page 71.

You wake up with the taste of sand in your mouth. Groping for solid earth, you place your palms flat against burning hot desert sand. You look back over your shoulder, afraid the white light is still there; you realize it's only the sun.

Go on to the next page.

You get to your feet. There is nothing but rolling sand dunes all around you, smooth as silk, untouched by anything but the sculpting wind. The dunes stretch as far as your eye can see, their light brown color contrasting against a pure blue sky.

You start to walk, feeling somehow that you know which way to go. Your head is heavy, but your feet are still light. You walk up and down the dunes, the white sun burning above. You travel long and far, until one day you see a looming black cloud on the horizon. You know you can't run away from it, so you wait. Soon it sweeps in on you.

It is not just a black cloud, but a series of demon sandstorms, each more powerful than the last. The wind wails, pelting your body with driven sand. You cover your head and mouth and keep walking, thinking you hear crazy laughter. As each storm approaches, you see in it a leering face.

After the last storm has passed, you find yourself crossing an endless grassy plain. You travel a long way on the plain, wondering about the huge dark blotches on the horizon. When you come closer, you see that they are herds of cattle.

One day a long roll of thunder comes from off in the distance. As a gigantic cloud of dust moves toward you, the thunder grows louder. All of a sudden a stampeding herd is upon you.

Turn to page 9.

62

You sit down with the zither across your knees and begin to play. You're amazed by the feel of the strings. They seem to come alive and dance on your fingers, making a stirring sound like none you've heard before. Haunting melodies and mysterious chords come from the instrument, which you seem to know how to play instinctively.

You close your eyes and lose yourself in the swirl of tones and colors. You're transported across canyons and deserts, soaring over bare mountain ridges and huge empty basins. You see glittering hordes of horsemen galloping across the steppes, great curved swords flashing in battle, heroic deeds, tragic love affairs, magnificent palaces and courts.

At some point you hear a voice, which you realize is your own. Your fingers slow down their playing, and gradually the last ringing chord of the strings dies out. But there is another sound, this one like rain. A strong, spicy scent hangs in the air, mixed with perfume.

You open your eyes, astonished to see all kinds of people gathered around you, clapping. They are the most amazing collection of people you've ever seen. There are jeweled women in veils, fierce men in baggy Turkish pants, pashas in bulbous hats, nomads, warriors, ornamented princes, and sun-burnished voyagers.

You stare with wide eyes at them as the words "What are *you* doing here?" slip out of your mouth.

Turn to page 26.

You stand up, holding your lamp. "Where would I find this door?"

Burton gestures all around. "Anywhere. As you can see, it is not a large space."

Taking your lamp, you make a circuit of the chamber. The perimeter is shadowy, but your lamp helps you see. Everyone watches in silence.

"Here," you say, tracing the faint outline of a small door on the far side of the room. You hold your lamp closer and find a tiny ring set into the door. You pull it open a few inches with surprising ease.

Burton, who is behind you, lets out a slow breath.

"Where does it go?" you ask.

"You will have to tell us," he answers. "Since we coveted the lamp so ardently, we could not find the door. As long as we still want it, we are unable to leave. But you can. Incredible things may await you. You may even find the Lamp of Aladdin. Just don't crave it to excess."

"I'll remember that," you say, pulling open the door and stepping through. "Thanks for your help."

Burton gives you a salute. "Good luck. And please—don't forget us. You're our only hope." As an afterthought, he adds, "Of course, should you *happen* to find the lamp . . ."

"If I should?" you prompt.

"Obviously, that would be the best way you could free us," he finishes.

Turn to page 29.

You can't resist finding out whether or not your lamp is magic. You squeeze the wick between your fingers. The flame goes out with a hiss. Immediately you're plunged into darkness. You rub the lamp furiously. "Come on, come on," you implore the genie.

But nothing happens. There is only silence in the chamber. You can no longer see your companions.

You try again. This time you massage the lamp gently, exploring its entire surface. "Come on out," you coo. "It's all right, no one will hurt you."

Still nothing. You squeeze the lamp hard between your palms and say, "I know you're in there. I command you to come out!"

Frustrated, you set the lamp down. "What do I do now?" you ask your companions. But there is no answer. "Well, will someone at least turn on a light?"

When there is still no answer, you stand up and feel in front of you. You try to make contact with the people who were there just moments before; however, all you find is empty space.

Over the course of several minutes, you become aware that a very dim gray light suffuses the chamber. As your eyes adjust, you begin to make out the shapes of your companions slumped against the walls. A gasp of terror escapes your lips—they are nothing but skeletons. Cobwebs hang heavy on their ribs, and a few shreds of clothing still dangle from their limbs. A chill creeps into your bones as you now realize there is no way out.

The End

66

You stoop quickly and pick up the snake's body. The crusader looks at you in shock. You shake it at him, but then he starts to laugh instead.

His laughter quickly changes as the body of the snake turns into a sword handle. Out of it springs a huge blade that just keeps growing longer and longer until it nearly reaches the knight's breast-plate. He stumbles backward with a scream, trips over the canoe, and falls into the river. You're afraid he's going to sink to the bottom, but the water is only shoulder-deep. He quickly picks himself up and flees across the river as fast as he can.

You set off on foot back the way you came. Once you're out of sight of the crusader, you sit down on the riverbank to figure out what to do next. You empty your pockets to see what you have left. There is the pomegranate, and there are also the jewels you picked from the garden.

You put the pomegranate back in your pocket for later and hold one of the jewels up to the sun. A tiny image appears inside of it. Looking closer, you see the garden, and beyond it the hall of urns.

You hold another gem up to the sun. In this one you see the garden, and on the other side of it the passage that leads back to the underground chamber of the Byzantine church. In another gem you can see Millie in the church, searching all over for you.

Turn to page 20.

You don't relish the idea of getting the lamp away from these Assassin fellows, whose very name sounds dangerous, so you say, "Well, it's not so much that I want the lamp for myself as that I'm just kind of curious about it. I mean, is it for real?"

Razad says, "I've heard different stories about the lamp. Some say it has an Arabian *jinn*, or genie as you call it. But I've also heard that the lamp can entrap its owner. Instead of your possessing the lamp, it possesses you."

"That's just a fable," says a man in Turkish pants. "Besides, the genie is from Morocco, and the lamp was owned by a Turkish boy."

"You're both wrong," says a man dressed in Persian finery. "The lamp is not a real object, it's a metaphor, a kind of magic. It was invented by Persian mystics—"

"No, no. I should know because I'm a storyteller," the woman says. "If it's not Arabian, why was it in the *Arabian Nights?*"

Go on to the next page.

"Because it was stolen!" the Turkish man claims. "It originated with the Turks in the Kirghiz, and the rest of you stole it—"

"How dare you?" the Persian demands, stepping up. The Turk reaches for his sword. Soon swords and daggers are drawn all around.

"Wait, wait!" you cry. "It's only a story. There's no need to get up in arms about it."

Turn to page 31.

70

Kogilu laughs. "You want to take that on a horse with you?" You look at the zither. It's almost as tall as you are.

Razad regards you gravely, placing a jeweled hand on your wrist. "The zither must stay here while you are on your quest. Otherwise, it would be no quest at all."

Gesturing around the tent, Razad says, "But you may take any of the other implements you have brought with you."

Turn to page 98.

Reaching the top of the stairs, you stand before the temple. The life-size niche, carved in the shape of a shell, is empty. Somehow you realize that this is your temple, a place that only you know how to find.

You spend a while here, drinking in the air and listening to the waterfall. When you have enjoyed it sufficiently, you walk around to the back. You open a door there, which you discover leads back into the Byzantine church where you left your aunt Millie. It's as if no time has passed.

You may not have found the Lamp of Aladdin, but you have found your own lamp, in a sense. You don't *have* it, exactly, but somehow you know you are still inside it, ready for whatever else life may bring you.

The End

The next day, sure enough, your horse's leg goes lame. Luckily you are near an oasis. You stop at a fountain in the center and cool your thirst.

"Now what?" you ask Kogilu resentfully. "I'll have to ride with you on Kyrit."

"No chance," Kogilu shoots back. "I would never ask Kyrit to carry two."

You're about to say something about how Kogilu will just have to walk along with you when a feminine voice comes from the poplar tree overhanging the fountain.

"Where do you wish to go?" the voice asks as you drink from the fountain. Reflected in the water is the biggest eagle you've ever seen.

"The castle of the king Aladdin," you answer, turning slowly to look up at her.

"I know the place," the eagle says. "It is many leagues from here, more than there are stars in the sky. You would not be able to get there with a herd of horses, much less one between the two of you."

"So much for our quest," you say to Kogilu.

He signals for you to be patient. "How then can we get there, eagle?"

"If only you knew my true form, you would not call me eagle," she sighs. "But an eagle I am, for now. I can take you there on my back—but only if you will help me return to my true self."

"What is your true form?" you ask.

"If you had a magic veil, you could see it."

You pull the veil from your packsaddle. Holding it in front of your eyes, you see a woman with a beautiful face—but the body of a cucumber!

Turn to page 34.

Soon you are soaring over mountains and steppes, the air whooshing through the eagle's wings. Thrilled by the ride, you keep pointing out new and amazing sights to Kogilu, but he's hardly impressed. He still can't get over leaving Kyrit behind.

You come into a barren land of desert mountains and dry valleys. The eagle begins to swoop down on a lone mountain. As you draw closer, you see that built on top of it, as if growing out of the precipice itself, is a castle. You do not have to be told that this is the castle of the Assassins. It seems impossible to you that anyone could scale this peak, let alone build a castle on top of it.

Feeling nervous, you ask if the Assassins really kill people, as their name indicates.

"Only their enemies," the eagle replies. "They are known to secretly murder their rivals. But they are a persecuted religious sect themselves. They feel they must defend their faith with their lives."

The eagle sets you and Kogilu down on a tiny ledge just below the fortress. You thank her and give her the veil. Just as she wings away, you hear a clatter from up the mountain. You give a cry when you see a black-garbed Assassin team coming down the tiny trail from the castle, waving swords, spears, and lances in the air.

Turn to page 87.

You're stumped for a moment by this question. Then you remember your friends back inside the lamp. "I guess I'm looking for Aladdin's Lamp," you say. "Was that it back in the garden?"

"You do not want that lamp," the snake replies, then pauses. "What do you wish to gain from the Lamp of Aladdin?"

You remember Burton's advice and wonder if this is a trick question. Playing it safe, you answer, "To free my friends."

"Oh," the snake says. "That could be a problem." He pauses once again, then asks, "Was there a woman inside the chamber with you?"

"Yes," you reply, "a princess. Her skin was very white. She didn't say much."

The viper is silent for a moment, then says, "You see, that's *my* problem. The woman is actually the daughter of our queen. Your friends took her captive in the hope of exchanging her for the lamp."

"Does that mean your queen has the lamp?"

"She knows something about it," the snake answers elusively.

Just then a voice calls from the bank, "Ahoy there!"

Ahead of you is a crusader knight, outfitted in chain mail. You're relieved to see another human being, and one that looks familiar besides. He's waving you over with his sword. You pick up the paddle and steer toward him.

"No!" the snake says, raising his head and hissing sparks. "He is one of the bad ones. We must not stop for him!"

Turn to page 38.

The man drags you over to another painting. It shows the same boy cowering before a huge, muscular genie, who is emerging in a cloud of smoke from a small oil lamp. As if reading your mind, he says, "Yes, my friend, that is the fabled Lamp of Aladdin. Now let me show you something else."

He takes you over to a third painting, which shows the boy with his head on a chopping block, about to be executed. "Bad things may happen to those who get what they want," he says.

"But in the story, Aladdin escaped," you point out.

The man puts his face right up to yours. His breath smells of grass. His eyes bulge and boil as he says, "Yes, but life doesn't always work out the way it does in the stories."

The man then leads you to a corner of the chamber. Middle Eastern musical instruments of all kinds are stacked in the corner. Hanging on a hook high above them on the wall is a lamp.

Letting out a slow, lustful breath, the man rasps, "Could that be it? We'll never know unless we get it down. But I am unable. I cannot climb ladders, and in any case there are none here. Together, perhaps . . ."

He leaves off the sentence, showing you his yellow-toothed smile. The reflected flame of the candle dances in his watery eyes.

You want to try to get the lamp. But perhaps you should get out of here and find your aunt Millie.

If you try to get the lamp, turn to page 99.

If you'd rather get out of here, turn to page 46.

You're practically falling off the edge of your seat as the merchant opens a safe and pulls out—

"It's only a manuscript!" you blurt in disappointment.

The merchant lifts his eyebrows and says, "Yes, I thought I was clear—this is an original version of *Aladdin and the Wonderful Lamp.*"

You're speechless, but Millie is thrilled. She gently unrolls the parchment and inspects it page by page. She says nothing for a long while, then cutting to the chase, asks, "What would convince you to part with this marvelous document?"

A long negotiation ensues. Millie assures the merchant she only has a certain amount of money, and he assures her she is holding in her hands a truly wonderful object and his price is special only for her. Finally they conclude the deal, both sides beaming.

You're not happy, though. These scraps of paper seem paltry compared to what you had within the sight of your own eyes—the Lamp of Aladdin itself.

Turn to page 96.

"Let's take a stand!" you cry to Kogilu, slapping him on the shoulder and showing him the dagger. This seems to wake him up a bit, and he takes a fighting stance to prepare for the onslaught.

The Assassins come thundering down the trail. Kogilu steps up to meet the first wave. Valiantly he strikes down attackers left and right, jumping over them, ducking their swords, flinging them down the mountain, and generally bearing out his reputation as a fighter. You wonder how your little dagger can possibly equal his.

The second wave of attackers is too much for Kogilu to hold off himself. You unsheath the dagger and step up to meet an Assassin. As his sword comes down toward your head, you hold up the dagger to meet it and close your eyes.

Your attacker yelps in surprise. When you open your eyes, you see that his sword has burst into flames. He drops it as it burns his hand, then he looks at you in terror and flees back up the mountain.

"Good!" Kogilu says to you over his shoulder. "Now get over here and help me."

You stop gaping at your dagger and rush to join the fight with your companion. You fend off every attack with your dagger, causing your opponents' swords and lances to burst into flames. Soon you go on the attack yourself, igniting weapons all over the place. The fight becomes a rout as you and Kogilu chase the Assassins back up to their castle.

Turn to page 105.

Rukn considers for a while before speaking. "No, the lamp still exists, as far as I know. I do not have it, but I may be able to tell you where it is—if you will help us."

"How can we help you?"

He looks at your bag. "Your magical dagger," he says. "We need it. Otherwise we may not survive."

You look at Kogilu in panic. "Why do you need the dagger?" you ask Rukn.

"The Mongol horde," he says simply. "They swept through here two years ago, laying waste to our fields and crops. We kept them from sacking the castle, but they were only a warm-up horde. The true horde is yet to come, led by Genghis Khan's prince Hulegu. With the dagger, we may have a chance against them."

Figuring that your dagger has done its job, you agree to turn it over to Rukn. Kogilu nods at your decision. "Now, about the lamp . . ." you say.

"The Mongols," Rukn repeats. "In their last attack, a few managed to penetrate the castle. Somehow they knew about the lamp and carried it off with them."

"Gee, the Mongols seem to get the blame for everything," you say. "Are you sure the lamp's not still here in the castle?"

Rukn eyes you solemnly. "I give you my word."

Turn to page 93.

You get back into the canoe and float downriver, disconsolate over the loss of the viper.

Then you remember his last words. You decide to make it your mission to help the Serpent Queen free her daughter. You don't know how you're going to do it, but your lamp is still in the canoe and the piece of the snake's body is still in your pocket.

The canoe drifts downstream. You sit back and let it. Other streams join in, and soon the river widens. It flows through a gorge and then empties into the sea. Rather than float out to sea, you drag your canoe onto the narrow beach.

A slow procession of camels is coming down a winding path from the bluff above the beach. The camels, loaded with goods, sway back and forth in a stately rhythm. They cross the beach and continue right into the water. No humans are in sight.

Turn to page 35.

The combination of Burton's words and your own instincts tells you not to give up your lamp. It helped you find a way out of the last place you were stuck in, so you figure it will help you again.

You start searching the edges of the cavern for a hidden exit. Finding nothing in the garden, you move once again into the hall of urns. As you continue to search, the lid of an urn behind you starts to rattle. Turning, you see a small brown viper slip out from under the lid. It drops to the ground—and slithers toward you!

You back up slowly, keeping your lamp and its flame in front of you for protection. The snake keeps coming your way. There's no doubt he's after you. Finally, backed into a corner, you command, "Go away!"

"Don't you want to know how to get out of here?" the snake says in a high, hissy voice.

You take a cautious step forward, thinking you have finally gone crazy. "You talking to me?"

"I don't see anybody else around," the snake replies. "Come on and follow me."

The viper slithers between the urns, back into the garden. He stops under a tree, which you realize is the only tree in the garden bearing fruit instead of sparkling gems. The fruit is red and lumpy.

"Pick one of the pomegranates, but do not eat it," the snake instructs. "Put it in your pocket and come with me."

You do as the snake says. You're not sure why he's so confident, but you figure you have nothing to lose by playing along with him for a while.

Turn to page 41.

You don't want to get involved with such anyone as fatal-sounding as the Assassins. "I think I'll
just stay here for a while," you say to Kogilu.

The people in the tent lose interest in you after
that. There is a general murmur of discontent. No
one seems to know what to do. They mill around,
and soon arguments break out once again. Names
are called, and threats are made. There are so
many separate altercations that you can't keep
track of them all. The tent is in an uproar.

In desperation you pick up the zither. Once
again you pluck the strings. Remembering the glittering horsemen on the steppes, you sing about
them. Suddenly you're in the middle of a rumbling
horde of Mongols thundering across a plain!

This isn't what you had in mind. You close your
eyes and start singing again. The first thing that
comes to your mind is the lamp—the one back in
the church. You seem to remember something
peculiar about it. It was hissing, as if it were singing. . . .

Suddenly all is quiet. You open your eyes. It's
dark around you, except for a small flame at your
feet. You're back in the chamber, the flame coming from the lamp you left behind.

You lean down to listen to the lamp. Strange,
whispering voices are still coming from the spout
and from the cracks in the stone walls all around
you. You decide to look for their source. Maybe
they'll lead to something more interesting than that
annoying group back in the tent.

Turn to page 112.

"Kogilu, what should we do?" you say in a panic. "We don't have a chance against them."

Kogilu, still pouting over his horse, draws his sword more out of habit than desire. "I don't know, but you have to make up your mind," he snaps. "Either we go forward or back. I can't leave Kyrit at that oasis forever."

You have both the bridle and the dagger left in your bag. You imagine the bridle would help you escape the Assassins, while the dagger would help you fight them. But you can't be sure.

If you take out the bridle, turn to page 104.

If you take out the dagger, turn to page 81.

You straggle back to the tent. It is deserted now, and all the objects are half-buried in sand. Wearily you dig out the zither. You summon all your strength to sing a song about going home, and pass out before you're finished.

You awaken to find yourself on the floor of your own bedroom in your parents' house. You're relieved, and after a quick tour of the house, you find that no one is home. After the longest, hottest shower you've ever had, you try to remember the name of the Turkish hotel where you were staying with your aunt Millie so you can call her. You have a feeling she's the only one who will understand.

The End

"Above this plain there is a pond in the hills," Balulam says. "They say that the water from the pond can heal an animal. But so far it hasn't helped my poor Kalika at all."

Balulam provides you and Kogilu with a tent and more food than you can eat. The next morning the two of you head up into the hills and over to the pond. There you find it, in a quiet hollow set among a few laurel trees.

You have your bridle with you. So far it hasn't done you much good. "Maybe you've been using it the wrong way," Kogilu suggests.

You play around with it, even putting it on yourself and Kogilu. Still nothing happens. Suddenly you remember the painting in the stone chamber. You run down to the pond, strike it once with the bridle, then step back and wait.

Go on to the next page.

The surface of the pond buckles, and suddenly a luminous white horse emerges from the water. You hold the bridle up, and it walks right into it. Kogilu's eyes are wide. "That's the most beautiful horse I've ever seen," he says, green with jealousy.

Draped over the horse's back are two canvas buckets full of water. "These must be for Kalika," you say. "Let's take them down to Balulam."

Go on to the next page.

92

You lead the horse back into the Mongol's camp. People gape as you walk by. Even Balulam takes in a sharp breath when he sees your horse. You remove the buckets of water and take them to Kalika.

Kalika slurps the buckets dry. Within minutes, she has regained her health. "It is a miracle!" Balulam cries joyously. He grabs you and hugs you over and over. Then, just as magically as it appeared, your horse disappears.

Turn to page 115.

You and Kogilu are given comfortable feather beds for the night, but you are unable to sleep. You lie staring at the ceiling. Rukn has given you his latest intelligence on the location of the Mongol horde and their leader, Balulam. But you are nervous about tracking him down. All you have left is your bridle, and you fear that to face such a foe you will need more, such as the dagger.

You have not yet turned the dagger over to Rukn. Now you wonder if you should double-cross him and keep it. So long as you have it, you think, the Assassins cannot harm you. In fact, maybe you can get up right now and make a secret midnight search of the castle, just to make sure the lamp is not here.

If you get up to have a look around the castle, turn to page 101.

If you decide to honor your deal with Rukn, turn to page 47.

You decide to put the genie to the test. "I want a pile of gold," you order.

"At once, O magnificent one," he says. Instantly pieces of gold begin piling up around you. They accumulate so fast that you are soon knee-deep, then thigh-deep, then up to your chest in gold. You can't move. "Stop!" you command.

The chinking of gold stops abruptly. "Take it away," you order. And the gold is suddenly gone.

"Anything else?" the genie asks.

Obviously you have summoned a very contrary genie. Thinking you'd better take care of first things first, you order, "Release the people trapped inside the lamp at once."

The genie bows and says, "It is done." You look around and ask, "Well, where are they?"

"One's in China, one's in Egypt—"

"Bring them to this cavern!" you order.

A moment later you hear horrible screams coming from the hall of the urns. You rush out to see each of your former companions stuck inside a viper-filled urn. "Put them back!" you cry.

The screams cease. You pant for breath. It appears that your genie is more than just contrary, he's malicious.

Turn to page 22.

96

You try to act cheerful for Millie, however, who is beside herself with excitement. Back at your hotel, you have an idea. "Maybe this isn't the standard version," you suggest. "Maybe it has something about the secret chamber and the lamp itself. . . ."

Millie knows enough Arabic to sit down and read the manuscript through. When she's finished, she gives you a sympathetic look. "There are some interesting variations on Burton's version," she tells you, "but nothing of what you're looking for. Sorry."

You sigh and think that maybe you'll go back for that goatskin jacket after all. Maybe that will cheer you up.

The End

The next morning you sleep late and, a little groggy, mount your new steed, bidding farewell to the Mongols. There's even room for Kogilu behind you. Balulam wishes you well on your journey, and you gallop off.

The speedy stallion has you back at the oasis in no time. After a truly touching and tearful reunion with his precious Kyrit, Kogilu turns to you and extends a hand.

"Congratulations," he says. "You have had the courage to fulfill your quest." You put out your hand, and the two of you shake heartily.

It is time for you and Kogilu to go your separate ways, so you bid Kogilu a fond farewell. As you ride off, you notice him looking back at you—or rather, at your horse. You think he is eyeing it a little longer than is necessary.

The horse gallops as fast as the wind, and in a few days you reach the walls of Istanbul. You ride through the city and back to the courtyard of the church were you left your aunt Millie. You feel certain she will understand, but you're not so sure your parents will believe how you came to acquire a gleaming white Arabian stallion on your trip.

The End

Following her braceleted arm you see that many of the objects that were in the chamber are here in the corners of the tent. Drums, flutes, and lutes are in one corner; bridles, saddles, and reins are in another; boxes, scarves, and veils are in the next; and swords, daggers and axes are in the last.

"What do I do with them?" you ask.

"Those setting out on a quest must always take their personal objects with them," Razad goes on. "Otherwise, how will you meet the challenges of the journey?"

You glance over the items in the tent once more, deciding whether or not you still want to go.

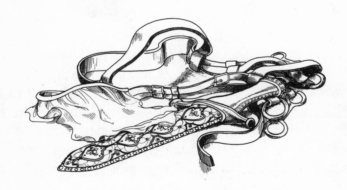

If you decide to search for the lamp with Kogilu, turn to page 111.

If you decline his offer, turn to page 86.

"How can *we* reach the lamp?" you ask the goat-man.

"Perhaps you can stand on my shoulders," he suggests.

You eye the man, who seems rather stooped and frail. "Are you sure?" you ask.

"Would you rather I stand on *your* shoulders?"

He bends down and hooks his hands together in a stirrup. You step up into them and then up on top of his shoulders, using the wall to balance yourself. He grabs your ankles and slowly straightens up. His shoulders are surprisingly strong and solid.

The goat-man shuffles toward the lamp. The lamp comes closer, and you reach for it. But as you grab it, you lose your balance. The lamp drops to the goat-man as you go crashing down into the musical instruments, producing a small symphony as they tumble over you.

As you dig yourself out from the under the instruments, you see the goat-man holding the lamp like a sacred object. You've never seen such a look of awe and delight in someone's eyes. He's like a child opening a Christmas present.

Taking the lamp between his hairy hands, he rubs it. It vibrates, and a fine mist comes pouring out the spout.

Out of the mist emerges a large, fuzzy brown creature. You can barely make out its little black eyes and small black nose under all its fluffy fur.

"I am the *jinn* of the Lamp of Return," the creature says in a small voice. "Whatsoever is your wish, I shall make it so."

Turn to page 13.

100

You look up, suddenly aware that the crusader is running along the edge of the river, yelling at you. You hand-paddle to the bank, where he reaches out to you. "I smote that viper just in time," he informs you. "Did you see the fire in its mouth? It was about to strike!"

You start to make a retort, then check yourself. You imagine the snake was harmless, but the knight didn't know that. And after the hissing voice of the snake, it's nice to hear a warm human voice for a change.

You wonder if you should believe what the snake said. What if he was just a demon sent to mislead you into thinking you could find the lamp?

You must think quickly about your options. On the one hand, there is the snake and his story about his queen and the captive princess. On the other hand, there are the crusader and your captive friends.

Which ones do you want to help—and whom do you think can best help you?

If you believe the snake, turn to page 43.

*If you go along with the crusader,
turn to page 107.*

You leave Kogilu snorning happily and start to snoop around the castle. There are plenty of lamps, but they all look too new to be the Lamp of Aladdin.

You are creeping down a corridor toward the central hall of the castle when a voice calls sharply from behind you. You turn to see two guards coming toward you, their swords drawn. You break into a run. They sound an alarm, and you call out, "Kogilu, help!"

You hear a door open down the hallway, and Kogilu comes running out. He distracts some of the guards, but more are filling the corridors.

You make a dash for what looks like open space ahead of you. You stop abruptly when you see that the open space is actually a sheer drop down the cliff of the castle. Drawing your dagger, you turn to face your pursuers.

Go on to the next page.

Six or seven Assassin guards approach you very slowly. At the sign of the leader, they sheath their swords. Holding your dagger in front of you, you command, "Stop!"

But they just keep moving in on you. You edge backward, wondering if you have the nerve to use your weapon on the men. "You need not—" one of them starts to say.

But you don't hear the rest of his sentence. One more step backward reveals that you were closer to the edge than you thought. As you plunge from the battlement, you let out a scream of terror.

The End

104

"I think we'd better get out of here," you say to Kogilu.

You pull out the bridle and throw it to the ground. Nothing happens, so you put it on yourself and then take off down the mountain. The bridle must make you fleet of foot, for Kogilu has a hard time keeping up. You grab his hand, and together you outrun your pursuers.

When you're finally out of sight of the castle, you stop to catch your breath. Only then do you realize that you're stuck in the middle of a barren desert that took you days to reach on the wings of the eagle. One look at Kogilu lets you know that you do not have to tell him this. He turns without a word and starts walking.

Even with the extra speed your bridle gives you, you must endure weeks and weeks of grueling travel before you finally reach the oasis. By the time you get there, Kogilu has stopped speaking to you. All he can think of is Kyrit.

With a quick salute, Kogilu rides away on Kyrit. He couldn't say good-bye fast enough. Likewise, all you want to do is go home.

Turn to page 88.

Waiting at the castle entrance is a stately man dressed all in black. He looks as if he might be evil, but his voice is gentle, and he seems impressed with your bravery. "I am Rukn al-Din, son of Ala al-Din, son of Jalal al-Din. What causes you to attack our sanctuary?"

You like the sound of his father's name, which is pretty close to Aladdin. "We mean no harm," you say. "We just want to talk to you about a lamp. Will you allow us to enter in peace?"

With a nod to his aides, Rukn al-Din has you and Kogilu escorted into the castle. You are treated with the utmost hospitality, but there is nothing lavish about the place. Once you see the spare, ascetic life of its inhabitants, you realize they lead a truly monk-like life.

At the evening meal, you and Kogilu are Rukn's guests of honor. There you have a chance to explain your quest for the lamp. After hearing you out, Rukn says, "My father was indeed the Aladdin you speak of—Ala al-Din, actually, meaning 'seeker of the highest good'. And there was indeed a sacred lamp, whose secrets were known only to a few. Where the wild stories you speak of come from even I do not know."

"You said *was*—is the lamp no more?" you inquire.

Turn to page 82.

106

Once the guard is out of earshot, you insist, "We've got to try to get in. You know I wouldn't lie about this, Aunt Millie. This is a really extraordinary place. Even if Aladdin's Lamp isn't in there, the whole chamber is amazing. You've *got* to see it!"

After some more badgering, Millie finally gives in. You leave the church, but at closing time the two of you slip back inside and hide in an alcove. When all the lights have been turned off, you find your way back to the door.

It's still locked. You've concealed a small crowbar in your jacket, just in case, and you start prying at the door. "Come on, Aunt Millie," you say. "Give me a hand."

You both pull on the crowbar, your grunts masking the sound of approaching footsteps. You look up to see not a security guard this time, but a Turkish policeman. He claps you into handcuffs and takes you down to jail.

A magistrate hears your case the next day. "I'm afraid I can't show you much mercy," he says. "You've been caught defacing a national treasure. You will be deported first thing in the morning."

You return, mortified, to your hotel to pack. Millie doesn't say anything, but you know she's mad. While she tries to figure out if she's gathered enough material to do her article, you try to convince her that the chamber was worth the risk.

"It really was incredible," you insist. "It was worth getting deported for." But your words come out sounding lame, even to you.

The End

You're sorry about what happened to the viper; he seemed nice enough, for a snake. But you're glad to be back in human company—that of a knight, no less. You figure if anyone can help you, he can.

The crusader pulls your canoe up on the bank and helps you ashore. You ask him how he has come to be in this place. "I set out at first on the Crusade—to reclaim the Holy Land from the infidel. But I was distracted from my purpose by rumors of a wonderful object, a veritable grail."

Something clicks in your head as you remember where you've seen the knight before. "Are you talking about the Lamp of Aladdin?"

Turn to page 51.

108

You go back to the doorway and wait nervously. The clip-clop sound comes closer. Presently a strange-looking man appears in the passageway. He's got a thick mane of unruly white hair. His shaggy white sideburns and beard, combined with his watery eyes, remind you of a goat.

"What are you looking for, young one?" he asks in a bleating voice.

Thinking that being honest is your best bet, you answer, "Nothing in particular. I was bored with the paintings upstairs and I found this staircase. I thought I'd see—"

"I'll show you some paintings that may be more to your liking," the man says. He rubs his hands and makes a snorting sound. "Follow me."

The man draws a candle from inside his large, rough-woven cloak. He lights it from one of the candles in the wall and leads you back into the passageway. It ends in a square, candle-lit chamber. Ancient-looking objects are stacked in every corner. On each of the walls is a painting.

The man grabs you by the sleeve and plants you in front of a lurid picture. He holds the candle up so you can clearly see the young boy in the picture about to be torn to pieces by a ghastly collection of beasts, including winged serpents, cats with elephant trunks, and wolves dripping blood from every hair.

"There are many different kinds of *jinn*—what you call genies. Some of them are helpful, and some of them, as you can see, are quite malevolent," he explains, chuckling.

Turn to page 78.

110

You decide you're better off forgetting about the chamber. You have only the word of the goat-man that the lamp was really Aladdin's. The thought of him gives you the shivers. You don't really want to meet up with him again anyway.

The next morning, right after your usual breakfast of eggs, toast, goat cheese, and olives—except this morning you skipped the cheese—your aunt Millie, true to her word, takes you to the Grand Bazaar.

The bazaar is an amazing place. It's like an indoor city, a bustling maze of tiny alleyways, each one crammed with small shops and stalls all selling the same thing.

"How are we going to find your man in *this* place?" you ask.

Aunt Millie just shrugs. "Serendipity. I'll follow you, you follow me, whatever."

Turn to page 10.

"All right, Kogilu, let's go find Aladdin's Lamp," you say, trying to sound enthusiastic. Everyone in the tent cheers wildly. Kogilu simply fixes you with his burning eyes and nods.

You leave your zither with the other musical instruments, but from each of the remaining corners you select one item. From the second, you take a bridle; from the third, a veil; and from the last, a pearl-handled dagger.

You make your farewells to Razad and the others, then prepare to set out with Kogilu. He puts you on one of his spare horses. Unfortunately it's considerably weaker than his own, which he affectionately calls Kyrit.

You travel a long way, across barren deserts and high steppes. "When are we going to arrive at the castle of the Assassins?" you ask Kogilu.

"I do not know," he replies. "I do not know the place."

"Well, how do you know we're going in the right direction?" you ask, exasperated.

"I'm going the way you told me to," he says with a shrug.

"What are you talking about? I never said which way to go!"

"When you got on your horse," he explains patiently, "you leaned in the saddle—your body said to go this way."

"Well, wherever we're going, we'd better get there soon," you warn. "This weakling horse you gave me isn't going to last much longer."

Turn to page 72.

112

You set the zither aside. Taking the lamp, you cautiously explore the crevices between the stones in the wall. As you edge along the wall, the whispers grow louder. They no longer seem to be coming from the lamp so much as they do from the other side of the wall.

The voices lead you out of the chamber and into the passageway. Thinking you can almost make out what they are saying, you press your ear to the stone wall. Suddenly the wall gives way, and you stagger through to the other side. You stumble to your knees but manage to keep the lamp upright.

Your spine stiffens as you get to your feet. Several pairs of eyes are now upon you. Slowly you turn in a circle, taking in the characters gathered around you. The only place you've ever seen people like them is in the paintings you've been looking at. Somehow you know without being told that one of them is a magician wearing full regalia; one is a Victorian adventurer wearing a coat, vest, and felt hat; another is a beautiful princess, her luminous skin and long black hair covered partially by a veil; another is a holy man, a Sufi, in a dark robe; and another is a medieval Crusader knight.

As you stare at them, you realize they are not really looking at you; they are looking at your lamp.

Turn to page 18.

"If what you say is true," you go on, "then why haven't any of you done it?"

"None of us had had the courage," the adventurer speaks up. You look at him, but he glances away, as if he has no more to say.

"There must be some other way out of here," you insist.

The knight eyes your lamp for a few moments. "Maybe yours is different," he says. For the first time you notice that the others are holding lamps similar to yours. "Maybe yours works."

All eyes are on your lamp now. You cradle it protectively. "How do I find out?" you ask.

"The usual way," the magician says and sighs, rubbing his hands on his cold lamp. "But first you must extinguish the flame. The genie will not come if it is lit."

"I don't know if I want to put it out," you say, remembering the trouble it took to light it. "What else can I do?"

The Sufi speaks up sharply. "There is only *one* way. You must go up there and dive into your lamp." You give him a skeptical look. He folds his arms and says, "It seems impossible, and indeed it is very dangerous. But surely it is the only way to escape."

You look to the magician. "If I put my lamp out, will I be able to light it again?"

He shrugs and says, "It is up to you—always up to you."

Turn to page 24.

You can't resist going after the lamp and summoning the genie. How can you lose with such power at your command?

After you have switched lamps and climbed back down the ladder, it takes only a gentle breath to blow out the lamp's flame. Recalling the story, you pour out what little oil is left. You're a little worried when it begins to burn a small hole in the ground, but your anticipation is too great to stop now. You take the lamp between your hands and rub it furiously.

Just then the lamp begins to tremble. You set it down and jump back as a huge billowing cloud of dark gray smoke pours out of the spout. Shielding your face, you look up to see a gigantic, bare-chested genie looming over you. He's got a big black mustache, fierce black eyes, and tons of chest hair in which nestle gold chains and pendants.

"Who dares to call me?" he demands in a booming voice.

"You—you—" you stammer. "You don't look like the genie I read about in the story."

"Who says I have to be?" he bellows, then spouts out a flame and a burst of laughter.

"No one, I guess," you reply. Bracing yourself, you add, "But you're at my command, aren't you?"

"You're at my command, aren't you?" he mimics. "Your wish is my command," he says with an exaggerated bow.

Turn to page 94.

That night there is a big celebration, with you and Kogilu as the guests of honor. For the grand finale, Balulam brings out the lamp. With a great deal of fanfare, he takes it between his fat hands and rubs. Billows of smoke pour from the spout, and a big, strapping genie appears.

"I am at your command," the genie says to Balulam.

With a flourish, Balulam turns the lamp over to you. "Anything you desire," he says.

You can think of only one thing. "Can I have my horse back?"

In the flash of an eye, the genie places the gleaming white horse before you. As Kogilu's eyes once again grow wide, you wonder if making him jealous was part of your motive in asking for the horse, even though you know you will also need the steed to get home.

As the celebration goes on into the small hours of the night, you grow bold enough to ask Balulam a question. "If you now have the lamp, why don't you just have the genie bring you all the wealth and plunder you desire?"

Balulam looks at you curiously. "What would be the fun in that?" What would we do all day? No, this genie is purely for entertainment. We're not going to let him put us out of a job."

You ponder Balulam's answer, and it occurs to you that he and his horde do not only lay waste to entire cities simply out of malevolence; raiding and plundering is their profession.

Turn to page 97.

116

One candle remains lit in the chamber. It stands beneath the fourth painting, which you now inspect. The painting shows a gigantic muscular man looming over a boy, who cowers before him. The man wears a turban. His arms are as thick as tree trunks and his brow bulges in anger. He is coming out of a small lamp on the floor.

A surge of hope wells up in your chest as you recall the story of Aladdin. But then the last candle flickers out, and you're left standing in the dark all alone.

You light one of your matches. Holding onto it as long as you can, you begin examining the strange objects stacked in each corner of the chamber. They look ancient, yet they are free of cobwebs and dust.

One corner is filled with musical instruments of all kinds. There are violins, lutes, drums, flutes, mouth harps, and right in front, a zither unlike any you've ever seen before.

In another corner hang bridles, saddles, reins, and other stable tack. Some are old and brittle, but others glow with jewels and garnets.

The third corner contains weapons—swords, daggers, axes, cudgels, maces, and other frighteningly toothsome implements.

In the last corner are stacked jeweled boxes, scarves, veils, perfume bottles, and garments of silk and satin. Wonderful scents come from this corner, reminding you of flowers and blossoms, and of your aunt Millie when she's dressed to go out for dinner.

Turn to page 16.

"No, you don't understand," you say to the crusader. "That's just an ordinary lamp."

"But we must discover if there is a genie inside," he insists.

"I've already tried it, and nothing happened," you say. "Now just put it down and let's be on our way."

But the knight is transfixed by your lamp. "Of *course* nothing happened," he says. "You must put out the flame and remove the oil first."

"It's not the Lamp of Aladdin!" you say, annoyed. "Now give it here."

You grab for the lamp, but he holds it away from you. "This may not be Aladdin's Lamp, but the genie inside can take us to the lamp we seek. Trust me, I've been doing this for years. I know a magic lamp when I see one. You must listen to those who are older and wiser."

He may be older, but he's waving his sword around like a child for emphasis. You're going to have to take drastic action to get your lamp back.

Your eyes fall on the body of the snake still lying in the front of the canoe. It's within easy reach. But so is the pomegranate in your pocket. The pomegranate is easier to get, and you're not sure what would happen to you if you picked up the body of the snake. However, one thing to be said for the snake is that it scared the knight.

If you pick up the snake's body, turn to page 66.

If you reach for the pomegranate, turn to page 27.

The genie looks down at you and folds his arms. "What were you saying?"

"Listen," you say, defeated, "I'll do anything you want. Just return me to where you know very well I want to go."

"Ah," he says, showing the gleam of a smile, "now that is what I like to hear from an owner."

You wonder what you're getting yourself into.

"It's a deal," he says. "Or is it not a deal?"

"It's a deal," you say warily.

"Deal," he says with a decisive nod. "Now, first I want you to gather all the precious fruit from the trees in this orchard and bring it to me."

Wearily you get to your feet. It takes hours, but finally you finish piling the gems in front of the genie. "The ones in your pocket, too," he reminds you.

"Okay, okay," you mutter. "Here they are."

"Now," he says, "go out to the halls of urns and remove all the lids." You cringe and stare at him, horrified. He stares back, unsympathetic. "They're only snakes," he says.

"What about our deal?" you demand.

"I said I would return you, but I didn't say *when*," he points out. "There was no mention of time."

Your shoulders sag. You don't have the strength to argue with him. "Don't worry," he says cheerily, "time doesn't really exist. When you do return, it will be as if you were gone for only a minute."

Somehow you have a feeling that *that* minute is going to be the longest one of your life.

The End

ABOUT THE AUTHOR

JAY LEIBOLD was born in Denver, Colorado. He is the author of many books in the Choose Your Own Adventure series, including *Secret of the Ninja*, the sequels *Return of the Ninja* and *The Lost Ninja, You Are a Millionaire, Revenge of the Russian Ghost,* and *Fight for Freedom.* He lives in San Francisco, where he plays catcher and first base for the Creeping Terror softball team. He is currently at work on a new series.

ABOUT THE ILLUSTRATOR

JUDITH MITCHELL was born and raised in New York City. She earned a Bachelor of Fine Arts degree from Chatham College and has also studied art at the Columbia University School of Arts and at the School of Visual Arts in New York City. Ms. Mitchell is the illustrator of *You Are a Monster,* and *Captive!* in the Choose Your Own Adventure series. When she isn't working, she enjoys music, animals, cooking, collecting antiques, and traveling. Judith Mitchell lives in New York City.